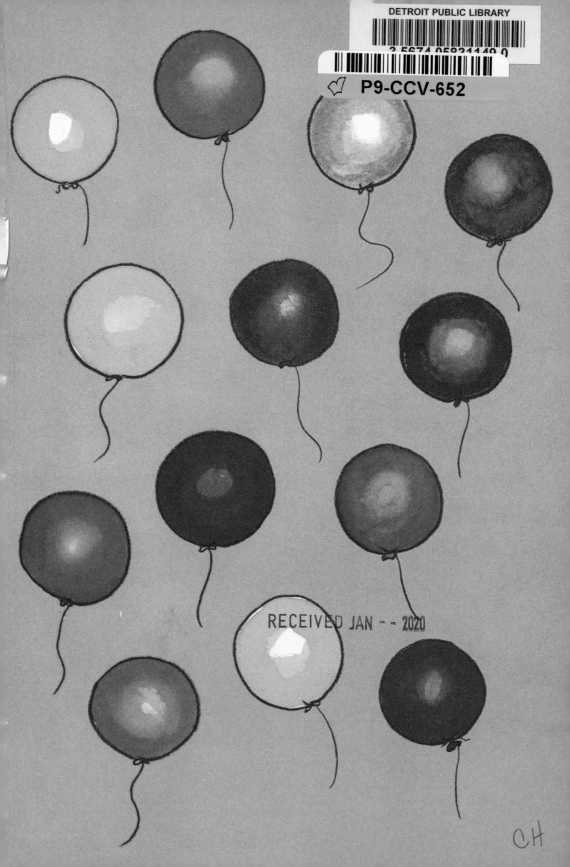

Joe and Sparky, Party Animals!

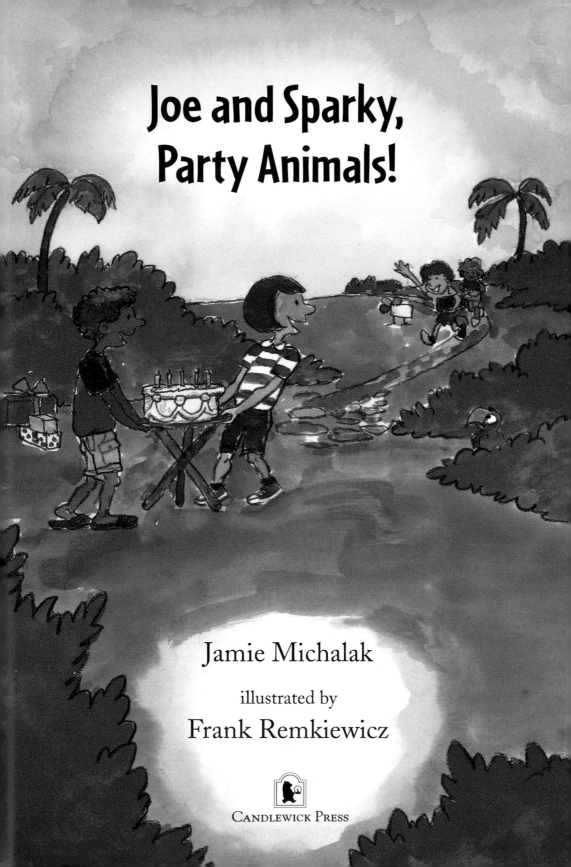

Joe and Sparky,
Party Animals!

Jamie Michalak

illustrated by

Frank Remkiewicz

CANDLEWICK PRESS

To Patrick and Finn,
and to Judy Michalak, the original conga queen
J. M.

For Hannah Grace
F. R.

Text copyright © 2017 by Jamie Michalak
Illustrations copyright © 2017 by Frank Remkiewicz

First edition 2017

Library of Congress Catalog Card Number pending
ISBN 978-0-7636-8206-4

17 18 19 20 21 22 CCP 10 9 8 7 6 5 4 3 2 1

Printed in Shenzhen, Guangdong, China

This book was typeset in Adobe Caslon.
The illustrations were done in watercolor and colored pencil.

Candlewick Press
99 Dover Street
Somerville, Massachusetts 02144

visit us at www.candlewick.com

Contents

CHAPTER ONE
A Surprising Idea

In Safari Land, the famous cageless zoo, a turtle hid in his shell.

Not far away, a giraffe stretched his neck to see the world.

"Hey, Sparky," said Joe. "Do you hear singing?"

"Yes, it is coming from that tent," said Sparky.

Joe read a sign. "THIS WAY TO SALLY'S SURPRISE PARTY.

"Slam dunk! A party," said Joe.

"No, Joe!" said Sparky. "That sign is not for us."

But Joe did not listen. He followed the sign to the tent.

Joe and Sparky saw noisy short people.

They saw a conga line. *Da da da da da HEY!*

They saw presents.

"Happy birthday, Sally!" the noisy short people sang.

"OH, NO!" Sparky cried. "Joe, look! Their cake is on fire!"

"Do not worry, my small green friend," said Joe. "I will save the day."

Joe blew on the fire. *Whoooo!*

He dumped water on the
fire. *SPLASH!*

He jumped on the fire. *Splat, splat,
splat!*

"Ahhh!" yelled the noisy short people.
They ran away.

"You did it! You saved them," said Sparky.

"It is a good thing we were around," said Joe.

Sparky nodded. "Safety first!"

Joe and Sparky walked back to the pond.

"I have an idea," said Joe.

"Uh-oh," said Sparky. "Your ideas get us into trouble."

"I will throw a surprise party, too," Joe said.

"For who?" asked Sparky.

"I cannot tell you," said Joe. "*That* is the surprise."

Sparky frowned. "I do not think that is how surprise parties work," he said.

"OK, I will tell you," said Joe. "I am throwing a surprise party for . . . ME!"

"Joe," said Sparky, "you cannot throw a surprise party for yourself."

"No?" said Joe. "Then I will throw a surprise party for Wiggy."

"Wiggy, your pet worm?" Sparky asked.

"Yes," said Joe.

"Oh, good!" said Sparky. "I will meet him at last. Can I see Wiggy now?"

"No," said Joe. "He is flying his plane."

"Wiggy flies a plane?" Sparky asked.

"Yes," said Joe. "When he is not racing cars."

"WHAT?" said Sparky. "I did not know worms could fly planes or race cars."

"That is the thing with worms," said Joe. "You never know what they will do next."

"I will make a to-do list for tomorrow's party," Joe said. He picked up a stick and wrote in the dirt.

EAT CAKE
LEAD A CONGA LINE
OPEN PRESENTS

"But, Joe," said Sparky, "these are things the noisy short people did *at* the party. First they had to get ready for it. They invited guests, baked a cake, and got presents."

"OK," said Joe. "I will get the present. Wiggy would like a twenty-foot necktie."

"That is about twenty feet too long," said Sparky.

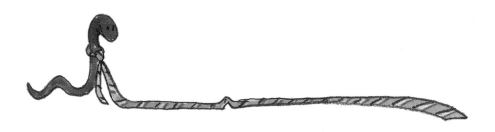

"Then I will make him a fruit hat," said Joe. "I will ask the monkeys for some bananas."

"*You* love fruit hats," said Sparky. "Worms do not."

"I will get Wiggy a basketball," said Joe.

"Joe!" said Sparky. "These presents sound like they are for you, not Wiggy."

"True," said Joe. "I will get *Wiggy* the perfect present. You can do the rest."

Sparky sighed. "I should have never left my rock this morning."

CHAPTER TWO

The Perfect Present

Later that day, Joe was holding a small gift bag.

"What did you get Wiggy?" Sparky asked.

"Guess!" said Joe. "What does a worm want more than anything else?"

"Dirt?" Sparky said.

"No," said Joe.

"A rotten apple?" asked Sparky.

"Wrong," said Joe.

"I give up," said Sparky. "What do worms want more than anything else?"

"Cool clothes," said Joe.

"Worms do NOT wear clothes!" Sparky shouted.

"Wiggy does," said Joe. "See?"

Joe pulled out a tube top, some one-legged pants, a belt, a hat, and one boot.

"These presents are all wrong," Sparky said.

"You are right," said Joe. "I forgot the underpants."

"NO! I mean these presents are silly," said Sparky.

"Yes," Joe agreed. "Wiggy does not need the belt."

"I have never met a worm wearing clothes," said Sparky.

"Well," said Joe, "you have not met Wiggy."

"Yes," said Sparky. "I am starting to wonder why. I see you every day, but I have NEVER seen Wiggy."

"I told you," said Joe. "Wiggy leads a busy life. Sometimes he is sailing his ship. Sometimes he is climbing mountains. Sometimes he is playing with his band, the Worms. They are even bigger than the Beetles!"

"Joe, stop!" said Sparky. "Worms do NOT sail ships, climb mountains, or play in bands!"

"I think Wiggy would like a leaf cake," said Joe. "Leaf is his favorite."

"Leaf is *your* favorite," said Sparky.

"The cake should be yellow with brown spots," said Joe. "It should say JOE GIRAFFE IS #1!"

"Gah!" Sparky cried. "Just for you, Joe, I will help you with this party. But I better meet Wiggy."

"Do not worry, my small green friend," said Joe. "Wiggy will be there."

CHAPTER THREE
The Uninvited Guest

The next day, Joe and Sparky were ready for Wiggy's party.

Every animal in the zoo came. The monkeys brought the cake. The hippo brought the band. The frog brought someone, too.

"*Psst.* Who is that guy with the smile?" Sparky asked.

"I do not know," said Joe. "But he looks like he is having a good time."

"When will Wiggy get here?" a hippo asked.

"Soon," said Joe. "Get ready to yell SURPRISE!"

"But I do not know what Wiggy looks like," said the hippo.

"Oh, he is a very good-looking worm," said Joe.

"SURPRISE!" a parrot yelled at the ground.

"That is not Wiggy," Joe said. "That is a caterpillar. Wiggy will be here soon. He went skydiving first."

"Skydiving!" said Sparky. "Worms do NOT skydive!"

"Wiggy does," said Joe. "He also loves to dance in conga lines. I bet he would like me to start one!"

"Oh, brother," said Sparky.

Joe led a conga line.

Da da da da da HEY!

Da da da da da HEY!

Da da da da da —

"HEY!" cried Sparky. "Watch out!"

A chicken tripped on Sparky. *Bawk!* She fell onto a zebra. *Oof!* The zebra fell onto a bear. *Grr!* The bear fell onto a lion. . . .

Roar! The lion fell onto Joe.

27

SPLAT! CRASH!

Joe fell onto Wiggy's cake and presents.
"Oh, no!" the animals cried. "The cake!"
"This is why you should never conga
with a chicken," said Sparky.

"What do we do now?" said Sparky.

"Want to play Pin-the-Tail-on-the-
Donkey?" Joe asked.

"No," said the donkey.

"Where IS Wiggy?" Sparky asked.

"Do not worry, my small green friend," said Joe. "He is on his way."

But the animals began to yawn. Only one guest seemed to be enjoying himself.

"At least *he* is still having fun," said Sparky.

"That guy is the life of the party," said Joe. "I will say hello."

"Hi," said Joe. "What is your name?"

The guest smiled.

"What kind of animal are you?" Joe asked.

The guest swayed.

"Hmm," said Joe. "Maybe he is the strong, silent type."

"I think he is dancing," said a porcupine. "I will dance with him."

The porcupine moved and grooved. Until the guest went . . .

POP!

"OH, NO!" Joe cried. "You killed him!"

"He is not smiling anymore," Sparky said.

"That is not an animal," said the frog. "That was a balloon. It was my gift for Wiggy."

Now nobody at the party was smiling. Joe looked nervous.

"Joe?" said Sparky. "It is OK if you do not really have a pet worm named Wiggy. You can tell me the truth. I will not be mad."

Joe did not answer. He looked at the ground.

"Shh!" he whispered. "Wiggy is coming!"

CHAPTER FOUR

Wiggy Was Here

"SURPRISE!" Joe shouted at the ground.

The other animals looked around. They did not see Wiggy.

"Where is the worm?" the hippo whispered.

"Happy surprise party, Wiggy!" Joe said. "Everyone, do you see how surprised Wiggy looks?"

The others shook their heads. "NO!" they said.

Sparky did not see Wiggy, either. But he did see Joe's smile.

"Oh, Wiggy was here," Sparky said quickly. "For a second. Then he popped back into his hole. He must be shy."

"Now what do we do?" said the parrot.

"We can still sing happy birthday," said Sparky.

"Yes!" Joe said. "You are nice to remember, Sparky."

The animals sang the happy birthday song.

"We can still dance, too!" said the porcupine. She moved and grooved.

The band began to play. The tigers did the tango. The raccoons did the robot. The animals danced all night.

"HAPPY BIRTHDAY, WIGGY,"
they cried, "WHEREVER YOU ARE!"

After the party, Joe gave Sparky a ride to his rock.

"Joe," said Sparky, "I have something for you."

He pulled out a present.

"A fruit hat? What a surprise!" said Joe. "I cannot wait to show Wiggy."

"Joe?" said Sparky. "I never did see Wiggy. Is there something you want to tell me?"

"Oh, that is too bad," said Joe. "You just missed him. He is taking a hot-air balloon to a place called Vegas."

Sparky smiled. "Right," he said. "Good night, Joe!"

"Good night, my small green friend!" said Joe.

On a nice warm rock, a turtle hid in his shell.

Not far away, a giraffe stretched his
neck to see the world.